LIBRARIES NI
WITHDRAWN FROM STOCK

D0433638

THERE'S A DINOSAUR ON THE 13TH FLOOR

Wade Bradford ～ illustrated by Kevin Hawkes

WALKER BOOKS
AND SUBSIDIARIES
LONDON · BOSTON · SYDNEY · AUCKLAND

"Welcome to the Sharemore Hotel," said the porter.
"You must be Mr Snore. Let me show you to your room."

"The sooner the better," said Mr Snore.
"I am very" – YAWN – "sleepy."

"Here you are," said the porter. "Room 104. Sweet dreams, Mr Snore."

Mr Snore thanked the porter, got ready for bed, crawled under the covers and switched off the light.

But as he was about to lay his head upon the pillow,
he heard a squeaking sound.

"Hello, front desk? This is Mr Snore in room 104.
Somebody is sleeping on my pillow."

squeeeak!

"Yes, that would be the mouse," said the porter.
"I believe he has had a very long day."

"So have I," grumbled Mr Snore. "And I do not wish
to share a room with a mouse!"

So the porter led Mr Snore to a room on the second floor.
"Sleep tight, Mr Snore."

Mr Snore crawled into bed and switched off the light,
but just as he was falling asleep, he felt a rush of cold air.

Mr Snore called the front desk again. "Someone is hogging all the covers!"

"That would be the pig," said the porter. "Shall I bring you another blanket?"

"No!" Mr Snore fumed. "I want another room!"

So the porter took Mr Snore to the third floor … where there were no pigs or mice to be found.

Mr Snore kicked off his slippers, crawled into bed, and was just about to close his eyes when…

Drip.

Drip.

Drip.

"Sorry about the leaky ceiling," the porter said as Mr Snore marched past the sea view on the fourth floor.

"This time," declared Mr Snore, "I will find my own room."

He found one on the fifth floor.

"I don't think you will like this room," whispered the porter.
"Unless, of course, you are fond of—"

"Spiders!" cried Mr Snore.

"Quick," said the porter. "To the lift!"

"How do you feel about bees?" asked the porter.

"The same way I feel about spiders," said Mr Snore.
"Please skip the sixth floor."

The seventh floor was too hot. The eighth floor was too cold.
The ninth floor was just —

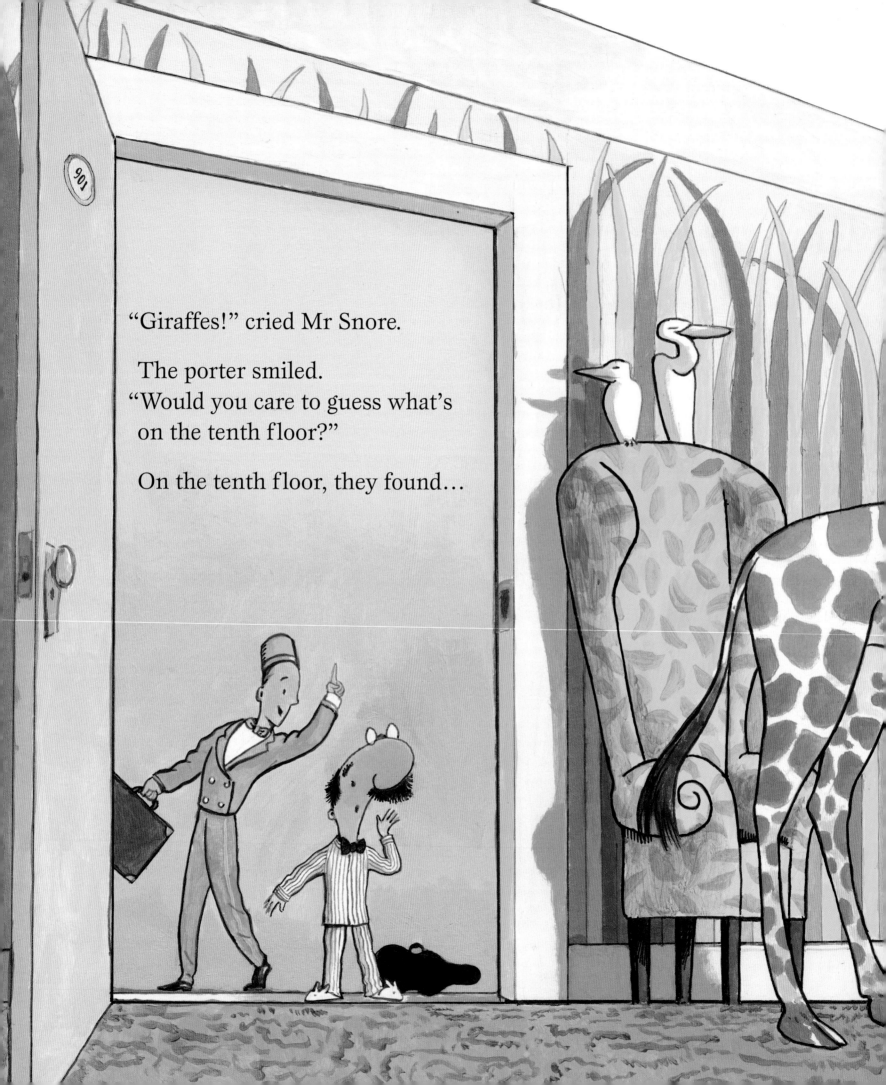

"Giraffes!" cried Mr Snore.

The porter smiled.
"Would you care to guess what's
on the tenth floor?"

On the tenth floor, they found…

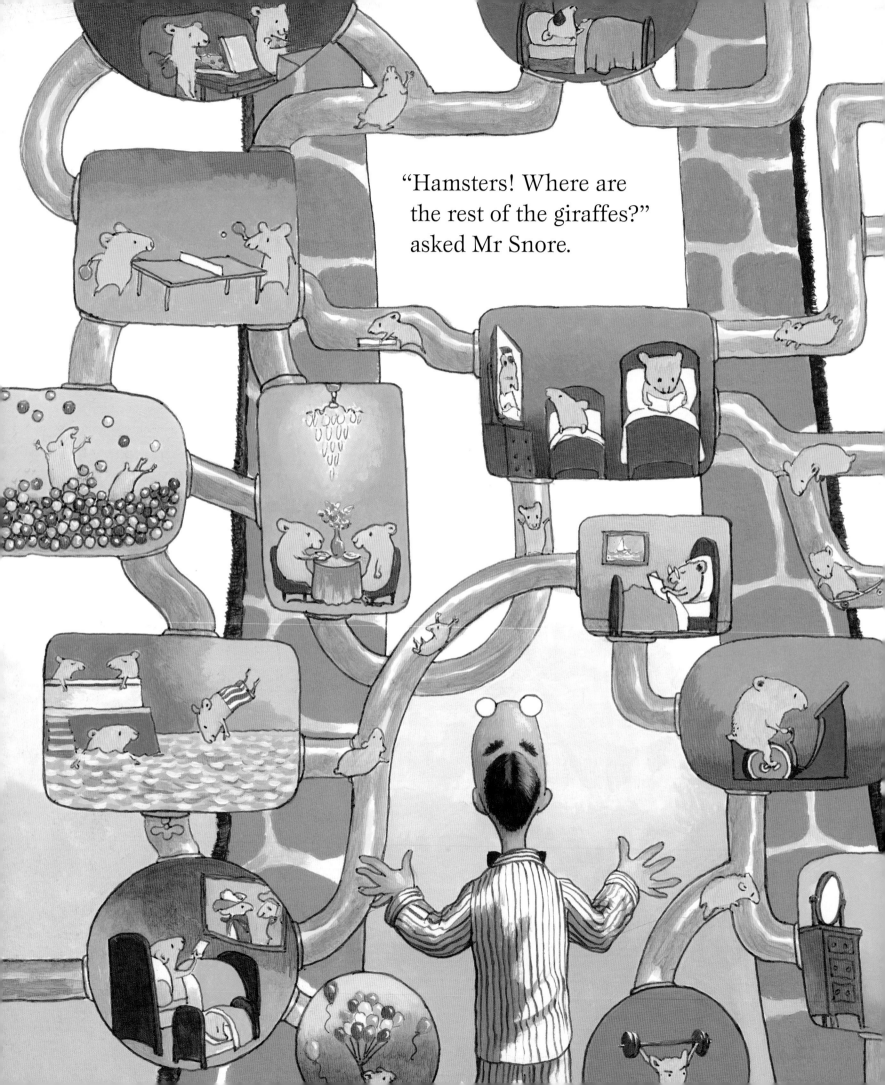

"Hamsters! Where are
the rest of the giraffes?"
asked Mr Snore.

"On the eleventh floor," said the porter.

"Then I will stay on the twelfth," said Mr Snore.

So they went to the twelfth floor. "Hey, it's empty,"
said Mr Snore.

"No one ever stays here," explained the porter.

"Perfect," said Mr Snore, and he lay down and shut his eyes.

"It does tend to get a bit noisy," the porter warned,
but Mr Snore was already fast asleep.

STOMP,
STOMP,
STOMP!
Gurgle,
Gurgle.
SWISH,
SWISH.

Mr Snore rang the front desk.

"I cannot sleep with all this noise! I'm going to find a room on the thirteenth floor."

"Oh, dear, no!" said the porter. "On the thirteenth floor there is a—"

Click!

Mr Snore did not wait to hear the porter's warning.
He went up to the thirteenth floor.

There were no mice, no pigs, no penguins, no snakes,
no spiders, no dolphins, no bees and no giraffes.
Not even a hint of a hamster.

Nothing but a giant room with a giant bed and a giant pillow.

"I do hope Mr Snore will be all right,"
said the porter.

Ring! went the phone at the front desk
of the Sharemore Hotel.

"Hello. This is the dinosaur on the thirteenth floor.
Somebody is sleeping on my pillow!"

The porter sighed. "That would be Mr Snore,"
he said. "He has had a very long day."